BRUNO'S BOX

By Nicola Pontin

Albury Children's

My name is Bruno and this is my box.

It's the
best
box
in the
world.

It's not just a box though...

I can be a bus driver

I can be a **pirate**

or an astronaut!

I can even be a huge

dinosaur!

It's the
best box
in the world.

But now my
box has gone.

And I
can't find
it anywhere.

But look what
I've found...

...a telescope!

I can be
whatever I like!

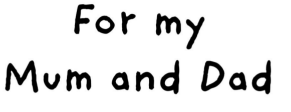

For my Mum and Dad

This edition published in 2016
by Albury Books

Albury Court
Thame
Oxfordshire
OX9 2LP

Text and illustrations © Nicola Pontin 2011

The right of Nicola Pontin to be identified
as the author and illustrator of this work has been
asserted by her in accordance with the Copyright,
Designs and Patents Act, 1988

1 2 3 4 5 6 7 8 9 10

ISBN: 978-1-909958-86-9 (paperback)

Printed in China